ANIMAL
EMERGENCY

HIT-AND-RUN
RETRIEVER

HIT-AND-RUN RETRIEVER

EMILY COSTELLO

ILLUSTRATED BY LARRY DAY

AVON BOOKS
An Imprint of HarperCollinsPublishers

Library of Congress Catalog Card Number: 99-96358
ISBN: 0-380-81600-8

First Avon edition, 2000

AVON TRADEMARK REG. U.S. PAT. OFF. AND IN OTHER COUNTRIES,
MARCA REGISTRADA, HECHO EN U.S.A.

Visit us on the World Wide Web!
www.harperchildrens.com

For Lacey,
the newest Chestnut

• 1 •

Stella Sullivan was grumpy.

Somehow, summer was already over.

It was the first day of school.

Stella liked school—that wasn't the problem. The problem was Rufus, Stella's puppy. She couldn't stand the idea of leaving him alone all day.

So Stella was sitting on the kitchen floor, hiding her face in Rufus's fur and trying to pretend it was June—not September.

Rufus knew Stella was unhappy. He kept twisting around and licking her face with his tiny pink tongue. Getting licked made Stella giggle, but it didn't stop her from feeling grumpy.

Rufus was a small dog—about the size of a Maltese or a miniature poodle. Nobody was exactly sure what breed he was because he had been abandoned at a rest stop when he was just two weeks old.

Stella had adopted Rufus right around the time school let out that spring. They had spent practically the whole summer together. Over the summer, Rufus had grown into a sleek, healthy dog.

"Come eat your cereal, Muffin," Stella's mom, Norma, said from her spot at the kitchen table. "You don't want to be late."

"Why not?" asked Cora, Stella's big sister. "I want to be late."

"I'm not going to school," Stella said. "Rufus will die of loneliness without me."

Norma sighed and yawned. "Don't be so dramatic so early in the morning," she said. "Come on, Stella. Get a move on. You only have ten minutes to eat."

"What about Rufus?"

"He'll be fine for a few hours while you're at school," Norma said.

"Cereal," Stella's dad, Jack, said. "Now."

Reluctantly, Stella went to sit at the table. She ate, made her lunch, and put on her shoes. The very last thing Stella did before leaving was give Rufus a kiss on his sweet furry face.

"Be a good dog," she told him. "I'll be home right after school."

Rufus trotted after Stella to the kitchen door. Stella stepped outside.

Rufus tried to follow.

Stella pushed the dog back with her toe and quickly slammed the door. She could hear Rufus barking sharply as she galloped down the back steps and pulled her bike out of the shed.

It was a sad bark.

School stinks, Stella thought. But she steeled herself, hopped on her bike, and headed toward school.

Route 2A was peaceful in the early-morning sunshine. The leaves on the aspen trees that lined the road were still green.

Stella rode down to the junction and stopped at the stop sign. Trucks and RVs were whipping down Route 98—the road that led into town.

Stella made the right turn, being careful to stay on the shoulder of the road. She stood up on her pedals and pushed the bike faster, anxious to get the ride over with.

Riding on Route 98 scared her a little—especially in the summer when there were so many campers and sport utility vehicles coming in and out of Goldenrock.

Goldenrock was the national park that surrounded Stella's hometown of Gateway, Montana. The park attracted tourists from all over the country. They came into Gateway to eat, buy groceries, or get fishing licenses.

Lots of the drivers on Route 98 went way too fast—even though the speed limit was only twenty-five miles per hour.

Stella rode hard for five minutes with trucks and campers zipping by on her left-hand side. She passed a sign that read WELCOME TO GATEWAY, MONTANA. POPULATION: 9,812.

Just past the sign was a sharp bend in the road. Stella followed the bend. A few feet further on, she spotted something in the road.

Stella slowed her bike, squinting at . . . whatever it was. Oh. A turtle!

He was on the double yellow line, facing Stella's side of the road. She could make out the yellow-and-brown dome of the turtle's shell. As she watched, his thumblike head appeared. Then four flat legs. He started to crawl slowly toward Stella—

WWWHOOOSH!

"Ah!" Stella screamed. She jumped back as a big white camper barreled down the road.

A moment later, the camper was gone. The turtle was still in the road.

Stella couldn't see if any more cars or trucks were coming. The bend in the road cut off her view.

She listened. She couldn't hear any cars.

Stella took a deep breath, dashed into the road, and looked down at the turtle.

He'd drawn his head almost completely back in his shell. And he had withdrawn his legs. Now Stella could see that the turtle was injured. His shell looked like a mashed M&M.

Had the camper that had just passed hit him— or a car that came before?

Stella wasn't sure.

It didn't matter.

What was important was getting the turtle off the road.

Stella hesitated. What if she picked up the turtle, and his shell fell completely off? Would that kill him? She couldn't remember ever seeing a turtle without his shell.

A low humming. A car was coming!

Stella dashed off the road.

WWWHOOOSH!

An enormous truck came barreling around the bend. Stella closed her eyes as the truck passed. She opened them cautiously.

The turtle was still there. Apparently, the truck had passed right by it.

Do something! Stella told herself. *Now.*

Everything was quiet.

She ran back into the road. Gritting her teeth, she picked up the turtle.

Nothing bad happened.

The turtle tried to pull his head inside, but that was impossible with his smashed shell. Poor guy. Stella hurried back to her bike and climbed on.

She cradled the turtle in one hand and steered the bike with the other. Two minutes later, she pulled up outside her Aunt Anya's animal clinic.

She left her bike on the front lawn and rushed inside. "Aunt Anya!"

Anya was Gateway's one and only veterinarian. That meant she was one busy lady. She spent most of her time on the big cattle ranches that were spread out across the county, giving vaccines to cows and caring for horses.

Pet owners brought their dogs and cats and birds and bunnies to Anya's clinic in town. Sometimes Anya even treated wild animals like owls or river otters—those were mostly brought in by Stella or Norma, who worked as a wildlife biologist in the national park.

Stella shared her aunt's love of animals, and she spent as much time as possible at the clinic.

"Aunt Anya!" Stella called again as she ran through the door.

"Stella—you okay?" Anya rolled out of her office and into the hallway in her office chair. She was on the phone.

"I'm fine," Stella said. "But I think this turtle is in really bad shape. He's oozing some sort of liquid."

Anya got off the phone and rushed to take the turtle from Stella. They hurried into Exam One and Anya put the turtle down on the stainless steel exam table.

Stella stood nearby, watching apprehensively.

"HBC, huh?" Anya asked.

"What's that?" Stella asked.

"Hit by car."

"Yeah," Stella said.

Anya pinched one of the turtle's rear toes strongly.

Slowly, as if he were moving through jelly, the turtle turned his head around to see what was causing the pain.

"Good," Anya murmured. She pinched him on the other side. Same reaction.

"Doesn't that hurt him?" Stella asked.

"Just a little," Anya said. "And it's important for us to make sure he's not paralyzed."

"Well?"

"Well, he has good reflexes—for a turtle," Anya said with a smile. "What are we going to call him?"

Stella relaxed a bit as she thought that over. Anya wouldn't name an animal she thought was going to die. "Is it a boy or a girl turtle?" Stella asked.

Anya shrugged. "It's hard to tell with turtles. Why don't we call him John?"

"John?"

"Yeah—after John Steinbeck," Anya said.

"He's a writer, right?"

"Yeah. And there's a turtle in one of his books. *The Grapes of Wrath.* A turtle that's trying to cross the road."

"Okkkaayy," Stella said.

Anya seemed pleased. "Read it sometime," she said. "The next thing we've got to do is to clean John's wound."

Following Anya's instructions, Stella got some 3 percent hydrogen peroxide out of one of the glass-fronted cabinets. She drew the liquid into a large dose syringe and gently squirted it over the turtle's wounds. The liquid ran off onto the table. White bubbles rose up through the cracks in the shell.

John craned his head around—trying to see what was happening. But he didn't seem distressed.

"What's next?" Stella asked.

"We'll need to let John's wounds dry out a bit,"

Anya said. "Give him time to rest. Then we can work on repairing his shell."

"Cool!" Stella said. She'd never seen—or even heard of—anyone performing surgery on a turtle. Sounded interesting. "How long do we need to wait?"

"Oh, a few hours."

Stella's eyes traveled up to the big exam room clock. 9:02. Stella was a bit surprised by the time. She wasn't usually at Anya's so early in the morning. She liked to sleep in during the summer.

Oh.

Oh no!

It wasn't summer anymore.

"Anya, I've got to go," Stella said, moving quickly toward the door. "I'm forty minutes late to school!"

• 2 •

Stella rushed outside. She grabbed her bike and pedaled toward the elementary school as fast as she could.

She pulled up to the bike rack, slid her bike into one of the few remaining spots, ran over to the front door of the building, and yanked it open.

Inside, the yellow hallway was eerily quiet.

Nobody was outside of the classrooms.

Stella's gym shoes seemed to squeak awfully loudly on the floor.

Still, Stella wasn't *too* worried. Saving a turtle's life was a good excuse for being late. Even on the first day of school. She was sure her new teacher would understand.

Stella knew where she was going. She'd been going to school in that building since kindergarten. Gateway was only big enough to have one class per grade. The rooms were arranged in order, with kindergarten next to the entrance, then first grade and so on.

The fifth grade classroom was right between the fourth and sixth grade rooms.

Stella didn't know her teacher, though, just her name: Mrs. Orne. She was new this year. Nobody knew anything about her.

Oh, well. That was about to change.

Stella flung open the classroom door and rushed inside.

Everyone looked up.

Stella saw lots of familiar faces. Her best friend, Josie Russell, was sitting next to Marisa Capra in the back. Jared Frye had gotten stuck right in front of the teacher's desk.

"Hi." Stella gave her new teacher a breathless smile.

Mrs. Orne did not smile back. She gazed over her thick, black glasses, slowly getting up from behind her desk. She was an older woman with straight black hair cut in a severe style with very short bangs.

Whoa, Stella thought. *Mrs. Orne looks like the mother from the* Addams Family!

"May I help you?" Mrs. Orne asked.

Stella felt like a bug under a glass. "I'm Stella Sullivan," she said. "I'm in this class."

"You are almost an hour late."

"I know," Stella said. "I'm really sorry. See, there was this turtle—"

Mrs. Orne held up one hand like a traffic cop. "I am not interested in your excuses."

"But I—"

"No buts." Mrs. Orne raised her gaze and addressed the whole class. "I don't like excuses. I like children who are on time. Every single day. Understood?"

Mrs. Orne's gaze returned to Stella.

"Understood," Stella said.

"You may sit right in front of my desk," Mrs. Orne said. "Where I can keep an eye on you."

Stella slid into the desk next to Jared. She felt like a criminal. And she wasn't thrilled with her seat assignment. At least she got to sit next to Jared. They'd saved a goldfish together over the summer, and they were getting to be good friends.

Jared gave Stella a brief smile and then went back to work on some sort of . . . test?

Could they have a test on the first day of school?

Apparently, yes.

Everyone in the room was scribbling away.

Stella watched nervously as Mrs. Orne went

behind her desk, picked up a stack of papers and brought them over to Stella.

"I've prepared some work sheets to test your knowledge," Mrs. Orne told Stella quietly. "I will use the results to place you in study groups. Work as quickly as possible. You're already an hour behind."

"Okay," Stella said, fighting back a wave of anxiety. She'd always done well in school. But she seemed to be getting off to a bad start with Mrs. Orne.

Stella picked up her pencil and started to read the first work sheet. Fractions. Great.

The rest of the morning went by in a blur of work sheets. Math work sheets, reading work sheets, geography work sheets.

Stella did her best to concentrate and make up for the time she'd lost. But after the long summer, the pencil felt strange in her hand. Her writing came out messy.

She was relieved when the lunch bell finally rang.

Stella sat with Marisa and Josie in the lunchroom. The three girls put their heads together and discussed Mrs. Orne.

"She's mean," Stella said.

"Not mean," Josie said. "Strict."

"Maybe this is just what fifth grade is like,"

Marisa said. "I mean, we're not little kids anymore."

Stella shook her head. "I think she's mean. She wouldn't even let me explain why I was late."

"Why *were* you so late?" Marisa asked.

Stella explained about the turtle.

Marisa's eyes were wide with sympathy. "Someone should do something about that bend. It's dangerous."

Stella nodded. Maybe *she* would do something.

"I'm just glad *you* didn't get hit," Josie told Stella.

"I was careful," Stella said.

Josie gave her a look that said she didn't believe her. "Hmm," was all she said.

School got out at two-forty. Mrs. Orne had assigned piles of homework—even though it was the first day.

Stella rushed outside and hopped on her bike. She couldn't wait to see Rufus.

As she rode home, she planned her afternoon. She'd take Rufus for a walk, get a snack, and then go to the clinic to see John.

Homework, Stella reminded herself. She decided to do it *after* dinner. She deserved a break after all those work sheets.

Stella was the first one home. Cora's school

wouldn't let out for another hour. Jack and Norma would arrive even later—around 5:30.

Rufus started barking as soon as Stella stepped onto the back porch. She opened the door and he bounced outside. The puppy was making a racket—barking sharply and running around in circles.

"Okay, okay, I'm home now," Stella said with a laugh. "Come on, boy. Let's go inside and get a snack."

Stella stepped into the kitchen. "Wha . . . ," she whispered.

The kitchen was a mess.

One of the white wooden table legs was scratched. Slivers of wood lay scattered across the floor. The newspaper had been pulled off the table and shredded. A drinking glass—which must have been sitting on top of the newspaper—was shattered. Rufus had tracked the spilled orange juice and something red all over the floor.

"Rufus!" Stella said. She turned and stared at the puppy.

Rufus hunkered down and looked up at Stella with a sad expression.

"Yeah—you know you've been bad!" Stella said.

That's when she noticed Rufus was holding his front right paw slightly off the floor.

Something red . . .

Rufus was bleeding! He must have stepped in the glass.

Stella knelt down and held her hands out to the little dog. "Come here, Rufus," she said gently.

Rufus took a step toward her.

Stella scooped up the puppy and grabbed his hurt paw. The largest pad had a gash in it. Blood was still oozing out. Stella couldn't tell if there was any glass in it.

"Poor baby," Stella murmured. She'd stepped on glass once, so she knew how much it hurt.

Still, Stella was a little annoyed. Rufus had plenty of toys. Why had he been such a bad dog? She'd only been gone for six hours.

She also felt a bit embarrassed. Training Rufus was her responsibility. Obviously she hadn't done a very good job. Jack and Norma would be upset about the table. And Anya would find out Rufus had been a bad dog.

Stella put Rufus down. She dumped her backpack out onto the now-empty kitchen table and put the little dog inside. She left his head sticking out and zipped the bag closed loosely around his neck.

Rufus didn't struggle. *Now* he was being good.

Stella picked up the backpack, gave the dog a moment to adjust, then put the pack across her shoulders. She went back outside and climbed on her bike.

Anya had office hours on Tuesday.

When Stella got to the clinic, the waiting room was empty. But she could hear voices coming from Exam One. Anya was with a patient.

Stella went into Anya's office and took off her backpack.

Boris, Anya's old basset hound, sighed as he got to his feet and waddled over to say hello. Rufus struggled to get out of the bag.

Stella unzipped the pack and put Rufus on the floor. The two dogs sniffed each other: Rufus eagerly, Boris in a bored, nothing-better-to-do way. Stella stepped into the hallway, closed the office door, and went to find Anya.

The door to Exam One was open. Inside Anya and a young guy were standing next to the stainless steel exam table. Anya was holding a ferret.

Cool. Stella liked ferrets.

Some people thought ferrets were big rats, but that wasn't true at all. Stella knew they were related to otters and weasels, not rodents. *Besides,* she thought, *what was wrong with rats?*

Stella knocked lightly on the open door.

Anya twisted around and gave her a smile. "Hey, Stella. Come in. Bud—do you know my niece?"

Bud nodded shyly. He was holding a tan baseball cap in both hands, nervously fiddling with it.

"Hi," Stella said. She recognized Bud. He worked at the gas station right in town. Stella didn't remember ever seeing him at the clinic before. His ferret must have been a new patient.

"Anya, Rufus cut his foot," Stella said.

Anya instantly froze. Her gaze shifted back to Stella. "He okay?"

"Well, it doesn't seem to be bothering him much," Stella said. "But it's bleeding a little."

"Where is he?"

"In your office."

"Okay," Anya said. "I'll look at him as soon as I'm done here."

Stella nodded and moved closer to the table. "What's your ferret's name?" she asked Bud.

"Freddy," Bud said quietly.

Anya was holding the ferret down with one hand and using the other hand to massage his belly. Freddy didn't seem to mind being examined. But he was curious. He kept trying to pull himself erect and see over the edge of the table.

The ferret had a long face with a mask like a raccoon. Small, pointy ears. Dark mouselike eyes. The way he stretched up reminded Stella of a river otter, but his fur was much longer and more luxurious. His two front legs were squat and shaped a lot like Boris's.

"Freddy is a very elderly ferret," Anya said. "He's practically older than you, Stella."

"Wow." Stella gave Bud a smile. He must have taken very good care of Freddy. Otherwise, the ferret never would have lived as long as he had.

Stella could see that some of the fur on Freddy's long, pointed face was starting to turn gray.

"So you were telling me that Freddy has been a bit sluggish?" Anya said to Bud.

Bud nodded, his gray eyes troubled. "It's almost like he's moving in slo mo."

"How's his appetite?" Anya asked.

"Not great," Bud admitted. "I even made him some chicken last night. But he wouldn't eat it."

Anya nodded seriously. She picked up Freddy

and handed him to Bud. The ferret immediately crawled up Bud's arm and sat on his shoulder.

Something about Anya's slow movements. Her gentle questions. Stella felt a stab of uneasiness.

"Anything else?" Anya asked.

Bud swallowed hard. He spoke quietly, as if he were revealing terrible secrets. "Well. Sometimes Freddy walks funny. Like he's dizzy, maybe. And . . . um, he paws at his mouth once in a while. At first, I thought something was caught in his throat. Like he was choking? But there never is anything there."

"I need to do a blood test," Anya said. "Freddy has to fast for four hours before the test. Why don't you leave him here and come back tomorrow morning to pick him up?"

Stella felt a low hum of dread. She could tell that Freddy was very sick.

Bud sensed it, too. "Um, sure," he said. But he made no move to leave. "Um . . . what are you testing?"

"I think Freddy has a type of cancer," Anya said. "The blood test will help me be sure."

"Cancer?" Bud inhaled sharply.

Anya nodded, looking sad. "Cancer is very common in ferrets. Older ferrets often develop tumors on cells in their pancreas."

"What's a pancreas?" Bud asked.

"An important organ that makes insulin," Anya explained.

"What's—"

Anya smiled. "Insulin is a chemical that controls the amount of sugar in the blood. Freddy goes into his dizzy act when his blood sugar drops."

"Can you fix him?" Bud asked. He sounded sort of choked up.

"There are some things we can try," Anya said patiently. "In my opinion, surgery is the best option, although it's not without dangers. Operating on older ferrets can be tricky. Also, the operation will cost a couple of hundred dollars."

Bud's eyes went wide. "That's so . . . I don't . . ." He trailed off, looking pained. Obviously he didn't have that much money.

"It's a big decision," Anya said quietly.

"It's also a lot of money," Bud said.

Anya nodded. "I know. And I also know Freddy has already enjoyed a long, healthy life. You can't really expect him to live much longer."

Stella's heart ached.

Bud looked so lost.

Anya reached out and touched Bud's back. "Let's take this one step at a time," she suggested. "The next step is a blood test. And until

I see the results, we can't be sure what we're dealing with."

Bud nodded numbly.

"Okay," Anya agreed. "Come back tomorrow morning. We can go over the blood test results and talk some more."

"I need some time to think," Bud said.

Anya made an apologetic face. "Okay. But don't take too long. Without the operation, Freddy will die within a few months."

"Okay," Bud whispered. He pulled Freddy off his shoulder; ran one hand down his long, furry body; and handed him to Anya.

Anya gave him a brave smile. "We'll take good care of him."

Bud nodded dully. Then he left.

Anya started down the hall to the boarders' room.

Stella followed silently. She felt drained. All her anger at Rufus was gone. So what if he was a bad dog? She loved him and she was happy he was healthy.

Anya lifted Freddy into a cage. She pulled out the water bowl and closed the door. She crossed to the sink and noticed Stella's glum expression.

"Don't feel too bad," Anya told Stella. "Feeling sad about Freddy is like feeling sad for a person who has lived a hundred years."

"But Bud," Stella said. "He's going to be lonely without Freddy."

"That's true."

Anya gave Freddy his water. "So," she said. "Let's look at Rufus's foot."

"Okay." Stella was ready to think about something other than Freddy. She got the puppy out of Anya's office and met her aunt in Exam One.

While Rufus panted happily, Anya picked up his paw and examined it carefully. "How did this happen?"

Stella sighed. "He was such a bad dog while I was at school. He broke a glass, shredded the newspaper, and chewed on the table leg."

"I don't see any glass," Anya reported. "I'll just clean this up and put on some antibiotic ointment and a bandage." She crossed to the cabinet and started pulling out supplies.

"Great," Stella said, feeling relieved. She grabbed Rufus's sweet face and kissed his nose. "I don't know what got into him."

"Well, you were off at school all day," Anya said. "He was probably bored."

Stella giggled. "Maybe he could come with me tomorrow and help me do my work sheets."

"Hmm," Anya said. She picked Rufus up and sat down with him in her lap. "Maybe it would be better if you left him tied up outside. That way he can run around and dig if he gets bored."

"Good idea," Stella said.

She watched as Anya washed Rufus's cut with hydrogen peroxide. That reminded Stella of the turtle.

"How's John?" she asked.

"Much better," Anya said, looking pleased. "So as soon as we're done with this little monster of yours, we can fix his shell."

"Excellent!"

"You know," Anya said, "John would have been roadkill if it weren't for you."

"True," Stella said with a broad smile. She felt good. She always felt good when she was watching her aunt care for a sick or wounded animal.

"Why don't you get our patient while I gather up some supplies," Anya suggested.

"Okay!" Stella went back to the boarder room and lifted John out of the old bathtub where he had spent the day. She carried him back into Exam One.

Anya was down on her hands and knees, rooting through a low cabinet. "Weigh him," she said.

Stella gently placed the turtle on the scale. "One pound, eight ounces," she reported.

Anya pulled a delicate drill out of the cabinet

and stood up. "Okay," she said. "Let me figure out how much sedative John needs."

She consulted several books and did a few calculations. Then she drew a bit of ketamine into a small syringe and injected John under the skin of one of his hind legs.

Stella inspected the strange collection of materials Anya had piled up on one counter—the drill, emery boards, needles, steel wire.

"You staying for the surgery?" Anya asked.

"Sure," Stella said confidently.

"Okay, then scrub up."

Stella moved to the big sink in the corner and started washing her hands.

Sometimes surgery scared her. Especially when it was on animals like dogs and cats. But mostly, Stella found peeking inside a creature strangely fascinating. Like discovering an unexpected alien landscape.

She didn't think operating on the turtle would be that upsetting. And she was curious about how Anya could fix John's shell.

The ketamine worked quickly. Soon John's head and legs were drooping loosely out of his shell. Anya pinched his toe to make sure he was completely unconscious. He didn't react.

Anya handed Stella an emery board. "The first

step is to roughen up the cracked edges of his shell," she said.

"How come?" Stella asked.

"That will help them heal faster."

Stella gently rubbed the emery board on one of the cracked edges. A little white powder rose off it—just like it does when you file your fingernails.

"Not too much," Anya said as she carefully fit a narrow drill bit into the drill. "We still want the shell to fit together."

"Okay." The sight of the drill made Stella slightly apprehensive. "What are you going to do with that?"

"Watch." Anya bent over John. She powered up the drill.

Vvrooom!

Anya carefully drilled a hole in John's shell about a half an inch from the edge of one crack. Then she drilled another hole directly across the crack from the first one.

"Doesn't that hurt him?" Stella asked.

"Shouldn't," Anya said. She drilled another pair of holes an inch down the crack. Then another. And another.

She moved on to another crack.

Stella was curious about the holes; but went back to work with the emery board.

They worked quietly and steadily for about half an hour until all of the cracks were sanded and drilled.

"Okay, next step," Anya said. She showed Stella how to thread a needle with stainless steel wire.

Then Anya used the needle to guide the wire top to bottom through one hole in John's shell, across the crack, and bottom to top through the matching hole.

She clipped the needle off the wire and picked up the ends. She crossed them, tucked one under the other, and pulled them tight—just like the first step in tying your shoes.

The wire pulled that part of the crack together, closing up the wound. Anya tied a double knot and clipped the ends of the wire short.

"Do you think you can handle that?" Anya asked.

"Sure," Stella said.

Soon they fell into a rhythm.

Thread the needle. Lead the wire through a pair of holes. Clip off the needle. Tie the wire tight. Cut off the ends.

As John's shell slowly closed up, Stella started to feel better. She was glad to see his ugly wounds disappear. And she always enjoyed working with Anya.

"How long will it take for his shell to heal?" Stella asked.

"Hard to say," Anya said. "Depends on how well he eats."

"Why wouldn't he eat well?"

"He's a wild animal," Anya said. "He might not like staying in a cage. And the stress could influence his ability to heal."

"When can we release him?" Stella asked. She was thinking about the other wild creatures they had helped. Usually Anya tried to release them as soon as they were well.

"That's going to be tricky," Anya said. "I'm hoping we can release him in time to hibernate. But if we have an early freeze this year, we'll have to keep him inside until spring."

"And keep him healthy all winter long," Stella said.

"Right."

Stella lifted her gaze and studied Anya's face. Her aunt looked worried. Probably because she was concerned about John.

Stella looked down at the turtle. The little silver knots they were making stood out against his brown and yellow shell. The wire looked out of place—cruel and man-made.

Stella knew the wire would save John's life. But it seemed wrong that he *needed* saving. In her mind, she saw the enormous camper barreling around the bend toward the helpless turtle. The driver hadn't even slowed down.

That evening, after dinner, Stella wrote a letter about John to the *Gateway Gazette*.

She showed the letter to her father who helped her tighten it up. Before starting her homework, Stella printed out the letter and signed it.

This is what it said:

> *Dear Editor,*
>
> *The bend in Route 98 just before the town line is dangerous. This morning, I found a box turtle on this patch of road. A careless driver had hit the turtle and crushed its shell.*
>
> *Drivers should slow down on this dangerous bend.*
>
> *The highway department should put up a big* DANGEROUS *sign.*
>
> *The turtle probably will live. But the next animal that tries to cross Route 98 might not be so lucky.*
>
> *Sincerely,*
> *Stella Sullivan*

Jack slipped the letter into his briefcase. "I'll drop this off with J.J. tomorrow morning," he promised. J.J. was the editor of the *Gateway Gazette*.

"Thanks, Dad." Stella knew her dad was good friends with J.J. She felt confident that J.J. would publish the letter. That gave her the courage she needed to attack the huge pile of homework that was still waiting. Someone should tell Mrs. Orne that homework on the first day of school was cruel and unusual punishment.

The next morning was sunny with a hot, dry breeze.

After breakfast, Stella led Rufus out into the yard.

"Arf! Arf!" Rufus barked in excitement.

The puppy jumped off the steps. He raced toward the far end of the yard where the grass was surrounded by a sturdy white fence. His little white legs were a blur as he ran to the fence and then doubled back toward Stella. His pink tongue hung out of one side of his mouth as he panted happily. His bandaged paw didn't seem to be bothering him at all.

"Good boy," Stella said when Rufus came back to her. She'd taught him to stay in the yard even when he wasn't on leash.

Stella reached down and clipped Rufus's leash to his collar. The leash was retractable. A hundred feet of bright blue nylon mesh rolled up inside a flat cylinder.

"Go get it, boy!" Stella tossed a plastic hamburger across the grass. As Rufus tore after it, she let out about twenty feet of the leash. That was enough to let Rufus run around the yard without getting too close to the forest.

Rufus grabbed the hamburger, ran back, and dropped the toy at Stella's feet. He was eager to play.

Stella ignored the dog. She was busy tying the handle end of the leash firmly around the handrail on the back steps.

Rufus waited patiently for a moment. Then he flopped down on his belly and started to chew on the toy.

Stella went back into the house and brought out all of Rufus's favorite toys. She filled his water bowl and brought that outside, too.

She surveyed her work. Looked good. Rufus had plenty of water, plenty of toys, and plenty of room to run around. He should be happy until Stella got home from school.

Stella got her bike. She dumped her books into her backpack and gave Rufus a good-bye kiss. She started to push her bike toward the gate.

Rufus stood up, suddenly alert. "Arf?"

"Sorry, boy. You've got to stay here." Stella pushed her bike through the gate and closed it behind her.

"Arf! Arfarfarfarf!" Rufus lowered the front of his body and let out a low whine before exploding into even louder barking. "Rrrrmmmmmm— ARFARFARF!"

Stella hesitated. Rufus sounded so unhappy. She couldn't leave him like that. She dropped her bike and went back into the yard. Rufus ran in a circle around her, still barking.

"Shhh," Stella said. She sat down and scooped him up.

Rufus put one paw on her shoulder and licked her face. Then he sighed and settled down in Stella's lap.

Stella spent a few minutes petting him. Then she tossed Rufus the hamburger. While he ran after it, she hurried over to the gate and slipped out.

"Arf! ARFARFARFARFARF!"

If anything, Rufus sounded more upset now.

Stella paused, holding up her bike. She waited—trying to see if Rufus would settle down on his own.

"Rrrrmmmmmm—ARFARFARF!" The puppy came to the gate and started to scratch to get out.

Great, Stella thought. *Dad will freak if Rufus hurts the fence.* Norma and Jack hadn't been too happy when they saw the damage Rufus had done to the kitchen table.

She dropped her bike again and went into the yard. "Rufus! Stop it!" she said firmly.

Rufus quieted down right away.

Stella went out through the gate.

"ARFARFARFARF!" Rufus started barking again.

Stella felt aggravated, desperate. How was she going to make Rufus stop?

She looked down at her watch. 8:15. She had exactly five minutes to get to school. The bike ride typically took ten minutes.

Stella's mind raced. Mrs. Orne was going to be mad if she was late again. That much was clear. She had no real choice. She *had* to go to school—now.

She peeked over the gate. "Rufus—shh! I have to go to school. Now be a good dog."

Rufus kept barking.

Stella took a deep breath and turned away from the dog. She climbed on her bike and started pedaling toward school.

Maybe Rufus will settle down once I'm out of his sight, she thought. *Maybe he'll get bored of barking after a while.*

Stella rode down to the intersection of Route 98. She could still hear the puppy barking.

She thought about turning back. But she knew that wasn't a possibility. School started in three minutes.

Stella turned onto Route 98. Traffic was just as heavy as it had been the day before. She made the right turn onto the shoulder, stood up on her pedals, and hauled.

Two minutes until school started.

On Stella's left side, cars and trucks and campers zipped by at thirty-five, forty miles per hour.

She rode past the town line sign.

Around the dangerous bend.

Straight into town.

Traffic slowed as businesses started to pop up on both sides of the road. Some of the drivers were looking for a place to park; others were just gawking at the sights.

The shoulder ended. Stella eased into the right-hand lane behind a rusty Ford pickup with Montana plates.

Past the gas station where Bud worked.

The rusty pickup pulled into the parking lot of The Wooden Spoon, a diner.

Stella pedaled hard, still standing up.

One minute until school started.

The clinic came up on Stella's right. Out of the corner of her eye, Stella could see someone standing on the steps.

She turned to look. It was Mrs. Jemson. She ran Clip 'n Curl, a hair salon on Main Street. A tan plastic animal carrier was at her feet.

Curly, Stella thought.

Curly was Mrs. Jemson's enormous gray cat. She had lived at Clip 'n Curl for as long as Stella could remember. She usually slept in a patch of sunlight in the store window.

Mrs. Jemson looked lost and worried. Stella could see that even from yards away. She seemed to be reading the sign outside the clinic. That could only mean one thing: Anya was out on a call.

Stella stopped her bike and pulled it up onto the sidewalk. She had to make sure Curly was okay. Curly was one of her favorite cats. She always let everyone pet her—even tiny little kids who liked to pull her tail.

"Mrs. Jemson?" Stella called from the curb. "Is Curly okay?"

"Stella!" Mrs. Jemson exclaimed, looking relieved. "I'm so glad you happened by. I've been *so* worried."

Mrs. Jemson picked up the cat carrier. Holding tightly to the handrail with her other hand, she began to ease herself down the stairs.

Stella watched nervously.

Mrs. Jemson didn't seem that steady on her feet. Stella had no idea how old Mrs. Jemson was. She was much more wrinkly than Stella's grandfather, and *he* was sixty-eight.

Mrs. Jemson's hair was pure white, but she wore it in an elaborate twist that she held back with rhinestone clips. She was wearing earrings and lipstick, too.

"What's going on?" Stella asked.

"Well, as you may know, Curly suffers from arthritis," Mrs. Jemson said. "Anya says it's to be expected in an elderly cat and I guess I can't argue. I've been slowing down myself the last few decades."

Mrs. Jemson pronounced her words slowly and properly, which made Stella wiggle with impatience. She *was* late to school.

"The stiffness hits Curly hardest in the beginning of the day," Mrs. Jemson said. "It just breaks my heart seeing her drag herself around so slow. She doesn't ever complain, but I know her. I can just tell she's in pain."

Stella was beginning to wish she hadn't stopped. She felt sorry for Curly, but arthritis wasn't an emergency. It would be best if Mrs. Jemson made an appointment to see Anya. Now she just had to figure out a polite way to get out of there.

But Mrs. Jemson hadn't finished her story and she wasn't in any hurry. "Then, yesterday, Mrs. Gould came in for a permanent wave. Now dear, you wouldn't know, since you have all of that beautiful natural curly hair, but permanent waves take a good long time to set. While Mrs. Gould was in the chair, we got to talking. Turns out that Hurricane has arthritis, too!"

"Hurricane?" Stella asked.

"Don't you know Hurricane?" Mrs. Jemson asked. "I thought you knew every animal in the county!"

Stella had to smile at that. "I don't think I know Hurricane. Is he Mrs. Gould's cat?"

"Heavens, no!" Mrs. Jemson smiled. "Hurricane is the most wicked little terrier you ever did see. Not that Mrs. Gould ever notices. She thinks he is *charming*."

Stella heard the school bell ringing. Mrs. Orne

was going to be furious. Well, there was nothing Stella could do about it now.

"Mrs. Gould always fools herself into thinking that Hurricane is just a little angel," Mrs. Jemson said, continuing her story. "Of course, Hurricane is practically fifteen now and he's too old to get into too much trouble."

"That's good," Stella said.

Mrs. Jemson nodded. "Anyway, Mrs. Gould told me she always gives Hurricane an aspirin to help with his arthritis. I thought I'd try it. Of course, I don't keep aspirin in the house. It gives me heartburn. So I gave Curly a Tylenol instead."

"How did it work?" Stella asked.

Mrs. Jemson looked troubled. "Not that well, I'm afraid. Seemed to make Curly sleepy."

Sleepy? Stella wasn't impressed. That wasn't any big deal. "Aunt Anya is probably out on a call," she said as she crouched down and peeked into the carrier. "Why don't you leave her a note and come . . ."

Stella let her voice trail off because she had gotten a good look at Curly. One fast glance was enough to tell her the cat was in trouble.

Curly's head was drooping and her tongue hung out. She looked as if she was having a hard time breathing.

Stella looked up and gave Mrs. Jemson a reas-

suring smile. "You know what? Why don't you come inside and we'll call Anya on her cell phone."

"Are you sure, dear? I don't want to take up too much of your time."

"I'm sure," Stella said firmly. She picked up the cat carrier, which was heavier than she expected, and started up the steps. Mrs. Jemson followed slowly.

Too slowly.

Stella had a bad feeling about Curly. She rushed ahead of Mrs. Jemson, unlocked the clinic door and pushed it open. In the door. Through the waiting room. She moved toward Anya's office, clicking on lights along the way.

She put the carrier down next to Exam One, went into the office and dialed the phone. "Pick up," she muttered nervously as the phone rang for a second time.

"Hello?"

"Aunt Anya! It's Stella."

"Hey, Stella. Where are you?"

Stella's heart sank when she realized that Anya sounded far away. Static on the phone was making her voice fade in and out. Stella had been hoping Anya was somewhere nearby.

"I'm at the clinic," Stella said. "Mrs. Jemson and Curly are here."

"Shouldn't you be at school?"

"Well, yes. But Curly is in trouble. She's panting and drooling and I think she's about to pass out."

Stella felt scared—like she always did when she was around an animal that needed her help. She didn't want to do anything wrong. She didn't want Curly to die because of her.

"Take a deep breath," Anya said. "Then tell me everything you know."

Stella took a breath and let it out. Then she explained about Curly's arthritis and the Tylenol.

Anya let out a low whistle. "Bad news," she said. "Curly *is* in trouble. Cats can't digest Tylenol or aspirin. It's poisonous to them. That pill could shut down Curly's kidneys."

"Is that bad?" Stella asked.

"It will kill her," Anya said. "Let's just hope it isn't already too late."

Stella's knees felt shaky. She didn't want Curly to die. Especially not like this. Mrs. Jemson would never forgive her.

"Where are you?" Stella asked Anya.

"In Billings," Anya said. "I was heading into town when you called. I just did a U-turn and now I'm heading home."

"How long until you get here?" Stella asked.

"Too long," Anya said. "Now listen, you're going to have to help Curly before I get back."

Stella heard a shuffling noise in the hallway. Mrs. Jemson peeked into the office. "Is everything all right, dear?"

"Um—just fine!" Stella gave her a brave smile. "I'm talking to Anya now. I'll be right out."

Mrs. Jemson hesitated for a moment, then withdrew.

"Ready," Stella said into the phone.

"Okay, you're going to have to induce vomiting," Anya said.

"Ewww," Stella moaned.

"It's gross, I know," Anya said. "But it's the only way to save Curly."

"Okay, I'll do it. But how?"

"Go into Exam One," Anya said.

Stella started to the next room holding the phone.

"Are you there?" Anya asked.

"Yeah."

"Okay," Anya said. "In the cabinet over the sink you'll find a brown bottle labeled 'Syrup of Ipecac.' Suck some up into an eyedropper. You won't need much. Maybe half an inch. Squeeze it into Curly's mouth. She shouldn't give you too much trouble about swallowing it. She probably feels about half-dead. Which she is."

"I have to put the phone down," Stella said.

"That's okay," Anya said. "I'm going to hang up. You can call me when you need me. Put Curly into the sink so she doesn't puke all over."

"Got it."

"Stella, one more thing," Anya said.

"What?"

"You've got to tell Mrs. Jemson what's going

on," Anya said. "Curly is very, very sick. It's not fair to lie about that."

"Okay," Stella said sullenly.

"Call me after she pukes," Anya said. The phone went dead.

"Great," Stella muttered. This morning wasn't turning out that well.

She took another deep breath—which didn't seem to help at all—and then went out into the hallway.

Mrs. Jemson was hovering right outside the door. She looked worried. "What did Anya say?" she asked.

Stella took another deep breath. Again, it was no help. "I'm afraid I have bad news. Anya said that Curly is very sick. Tylenol is poison to cats."

Mrs. Jemson gasped. Shaky hands flew up to her mouth. "Is Curly going to die?" she whispered.

"I don't know," Stella said, feeling cruel for being so honest. "But you have to be brave. Anya is on her way. And she told me what to do until she gets here."

Mrs. Jemson nodded. "Please do whatever you can," she said. "God bless."

Stella took the carrier into Exam One and put it down on the table. She pulled Curly out. Curly was such a big cat, she had to use both hands.

"Mrrrw," Curly moaned. She was limp in Stella's hands.

"It's okay, Curly," Stella murmured. "Everything is going to be just fine."

She put the cat down on the table and prepared the Syrup of Ipecac just like Anya had told her. She held up Curly's chin and squeezed the liquid back behind the cat's cheek.

Stella felt movement in Curly's throat as she swallowed. She quickly picked up the cat and moved her to the sink.

Just in time!

As soon as Stella put her down, Curly began to heave weakly. She jerked her head forward again and again. She made a harsh, gagging sound and spit out a puddle of puke.

It wasn't a pretty sight.

Or a pretty smell.

"All done?" Stella said.

Curly didn't move. She looked completely and totally miserable. Stella lifted the cat, rinsed out the sink and put her back down. Then she called Anya.

Anya picked up on the first ring. "How's it going?"

"Well, the Syrup of Ipecac—um, worked."

"Good," Anya said cheerfully. "Now you need to give her something to slow the absorption of

the poison. Look in the cabinet next to the syrup
of ipecac. You should see some little tubes marked
'liquid charcoal' or something like that."

"Got it," Stella reported.

"Okay," Anya said. "Shake and squeeze one of
the tubes for a few minutes. Then you're going
to have to put a tube down into Curly's stomach."

"No problem." Stella had put a tube into Rufus's stomach dozens of times when he was too
small and weak to eat.

"After the stomach tube is in place," Anya continued, "snip the top off the medicine and squeeze
it into the stomach tube."

"Okay," Stella said. "How long until you get back?"

"Another fifteen minutes or so," Anya said.

Too late to help.

Stella turned off the phone and set to work. She moved Curly onto the table, measured the tubing, and eased it down over her tongue. Then she prepared the medicine and squeezed it in.

Curly didn't put up any kind of fight.

Stella was just removing the stomach tube when she heard a sound at the door. She looked up and saw Anya rushing in.

"I thought you weren't going to be here for fifteen minutes."

"It's been almost twenty."

"Oh."

Anya rushed up to the table and examined Curly. She looked into the cat's eyes, felt her heartbeat, inspected her tongue.

Stella stood a step away from the table. She waited tensely. She was afraid of getting bad news, but also incredibly relieved that Anya was there to take care of things.

Anya let out all of her breath. "Curly looks like one sick kitty." She turned to Stella and gave her a smile. "If you hadn't acted, she'd probably be dead about now. Good catch."

Stella felt her cheeks warm up. She felt a

warm glow travel from her toes all the way up to her scalp. Nice to save Curly's life. Just as nice to have Anya's praise.

"Thanks," Stella said. "So she's going to be okay?"

"Well, I'll need to do some blood tests to make sure her kidneys aren't affected. But I think she'll survive."

"Great."

Anya was drawing a little of Curly's blood when Stella heard a shuffling sound in the hallway. Mrs. Jemson! Stella had forgotten all about her.

Mrs. Jemson stuck her head around the doorframe. "I don't mean to interrupt. But I just have to know. How is Curly doing?"

"Come in," Anya said warmly. "Curly is much better."

Mrs. Jemson clasped her hands together and turned to Stella with an enormous smile. "Well, I'll be! This child has a gift!"

"It was no big deal," Stella muttered.

"It was a very big deal to me," Mrs. Jemson replied. She came over, grasped Stella's cheeks between two gnarled hands, and kissed her forehead. "Thank you, my dear! Thank you!"

"You're welcome," Stella said.

Then she remembered.

School!

"Um—I've got to go!" Stella said urgently.

"Do you want me to write you a note or something?" Anya asked.

"No. No, that won't help. I'll see you later, Anya. Bye, Mrs. Jemson."

"Good-bye, dear. Come in for a haircut. My treat."

"Okay," Stella said.

And then she ran.

Ten minutes later, Stella eased into the classroom. Her T-shirt was damp with sweat. She was panting and her heart was thud-thudding.

Mrs. Orne gave her the look of death.

"I can explain," Stella said meekly.

"No excuses," Mrs. Orne said coldly. "I warned you yesterday. Now I am giving you a week of detention."

"But—"

Mrs. Orne held up one hand. "Please. Don't take up any more of our classroom time arguing with me. I can assure you I won't change my mind. Just take your seat."

Stella slid into her seat, feeling totally hateful toward Mrs. Orne.

There are more important things in the world than being on time, she thought. *If I hadn't been late today, Curly would have died.*

She knew that Mrs. Orne didn't care. And wouldn't even listen. It wasn't fair.

As Stella's anger faded, she started to feel apprehensive. She had never had detention before. She was nervous about what was going to happen.

School finally ended.

The other kids poured out of the classroom. Stella stayed in her seat. So did Duncan Crowe. Stella was surprised. She thought it was just going to be her and Mrs. Orne staying after school.

Stella had never liked Duncan much. He was always cracking jokes in class. But still—having him around was better than being alone with Mrs. Orne.

The teacher was at her desk, head bent over a stack of papers. She waited until the school had quieted down. Then she looked up and told Duncan and Stella to work on their homework until 3:00.

Stella pulled out her math book and got to work. She liked math—and knew it was important for veterinarians—so the twenty minutes went by quickly.

"You may go now," Mrs. Orne said at 3:00. She didn't even look up at them.

Duncan and Stella quickly gathered their

books and hurried out. Detention hadn't been any big deal, Stella thought. Still, she felt resentful for being punished.

"Whew," Duncan said out in the hallway. "I'm glad that's over."

They moved toward the door together.

"Did you just get detention for today?" Stella asked.

"Nope," Duncan said with a sigh. "All week."

"What did you do?" Stella asked.

"I was late. Two days in a row."

Stella laughed. "Common problem."

Duncan nodded as he opened the door. "I've got this calf and she will not eat. It's really bugging me because I'm going to show her in the county fair and I want a blue ribbon."

"Why won't she eat?" Stella asked.

"Too much junk food?" Duncan suggested.

Stella rolled her eyes. "What do your parents think?" she asked.

"They don't know," Duncan said. "Daddy drives a truck and Momma teaches little preschoolers. My uncle gave me the calf. He has this little dairy and says maybe I'll work it with him some-day. He doesn't have any kids of his own."

"Why don't you call him?"

"Momma won't let me," Duncan explained. "He

lives all the way over in North Dakota. It's a long-distance call."

"Maybe you should call my Aunt Anya," Stella said.

Duncan made a face. "Can't. I don't have the money to pay for a veterinarian."

Stella didn't know what to say. She didn't think people should keep animals if they couldn't afford to take care of them. But she didn't want to lecture Duncan. And he seemed really proud of his calf.

"Maybe one of your neighbors can help," Stella suggested.

"Maybe. Well, see you later."

"See you."

Stella hopped on her bike and pedaled toward home. Thanks to Mrs. Orne, Rufus had been home alone for an extra twenty minutes.

"Arf, arf, arf . . ."

When Stella pulled onto Route 2A, she could hear the puppy barking. When she opened the gate, he was all over her. Barking and jumping up and running in circles and rolling on the ground and barking some more.

Stella laughed. "Hi, boy! I missed you, too." She sat down in the grass and pulled the puppy into her lap.

Rufus's tail was going double-time. He put one paw on her shoulder and licked her face.

Stella lay back in the grass with a sigh. She was relieved. Obviously leaving Rufus outside was the right thing to do. At least one thing had turned out well today.

"Hello?"

Stella sat up and looked toward the gate. Mrs. Barber, the Sullivans' next door neighbor, was coming in. She was wearing sweats and a big gray robe. Her nose was bright red and she was holding a tissue.

"Hi, Mrs. Barber."

"Stella, I thought you'd be home. Honey, Rufus has been barking all day long. I had a cold and I stayed home to get some rest, but it was impossible with all the racket he was making."

Stella's heart sank.

Poor Mrs. Barber.

Poor Rufus.

What was she going to do now?

• 7 •

Stella was still sitting in the yard when Jack came home ten minutes later. Rufus was stretched out on his back, being a good, quiet puppy.

Jack walked through the gate, studied Stella's face for a second, and then went to sit on the back steps.

"Did J.J. call?" he asked.

"J.J.? No."

"Oh. I just thought . . . you looked so sad."

"Because Rufus was bad again. He barked all day long and bugged Mrs. Barber," Stella said. Then, "What about J.J.?"

"He refused to publish your letter."

"Why?"

Jack sighed. "He says nobody cares about turtles."

"That's not true!" Stella exclaimed. "And besides, that's not the point."

"I told him the same thing," Jack said sadly. "He wasn't impressed."

"Great," Stella said bitterly. "This has been the worst day of my life."

Jack looked sympathetic. "Why don't you come inside and help me with dinner?" he suggested. "Chopping vegetables always makes me feel better. And Anya is coming to dinner."

"Okay," Stella said, slowly getting to her feet.

Jack was right. Chopping vegetables *was* soothing. By the time Stella had diced a large onion, six carrots, and three celery stalks, her mood was starting to pick up. Of course that may have had something to do with the wonderful smells coming from the pan of meat sauce.

After she finished with the vegetables, Stella set the table. By a little after six, the Sullivans and Anya were sitting down to dinner.

"How did Rufus do today?" Norma asked as she helped herself to a piece of garlic bread.

"Not good," Stella told her. "He barked all day. Mrs. Barber was kind of mad." She turned to Anya. "Do you think Rufus is still bored? He had the whole yard to run around in. And plenty of toys."

Anya considered as she chewed. "He could be lonely, or mad about being left alone."

"What am I going to do?" Stella asked.

"I have the perfect solution," Cora said. "Let's get another dog to keep Rufus company."

"Yes!" Stella said.

"No!" Norma and Jack said at the same time.

Anya laughed. "I have another suggestion. Why don't you try leaving Rufus at the clinic during the day? That way he can play with Boris."

"Are you sure?" Norma asked.

Anya shrugged. "We'll give it a try. But if he's a bad dog, I'll kick him out."

"Cool," Stella said, doing her best to sound confident and grateful. Actually, she had her doubts. Rufus had been bad two days in a row. What were the chances he'd be good for Anya?

The conversation shifted.

Cora told everyone about school. She *loved* her new teachers.

Shifted again. Stella told about Duncan and his calf.

Anya listened with interest. "Let's ride out there after dinner," she suggested to Stella. "I'll take a quick look at him."

"Would you?" Stella asked. "That would be great!"

Norma gave her a look. "What about your homework?"

"I finished it already," Stella said. Then her guilty conscience got the best of her and she added, "During detention." .

Everyone turned to Stella.

"Detention?" Jack repeated faintly.

Stella sighed and told about being late and how Mrs. Orne wouldn't even let her *explain*. "She's mean," Stella finished.

Cora nodded. "Poor Stella. You're going to have to spend the entire school year with her."

Suddenly Stella didn't feel very hungry.

Norma sighed. "Muffin, it sounds as if you had some very good reasons for being late. But I'm afraid Mrs. Orne has a point. School is important, too. And you ought to get there on time."

"You think I should have left Curly to die!" Stella demanded.

"Of course not," Norma said. "But you made a conscious decision to be late. Now you have to take responsibility for that decision."

"A week of detention," Stella said sullenly.

"I think it was worth it," Cora said.

Stella smiled at her sister. Cora was right. A week of detention was no big deal. She would have been happy to stay late all *year* if that's what it took to save Curly. But she still thought Mrs. Orne should have let her explain.

When Stella and Anya walked out to Anya's 4 x 4 after dinner, the sky was baby blue. The few scattered clouds Stella could see were tinted pink by the setting sun.

Stella zipped her sweatshirt and pulled on the hood. The evening air was chilly. She thought of John the turtle. She hoped his shell would heal before it got too cold.

Anya started up the truck and pulled onto 2A, heading away from town. She'd called the Crowes from Stella's house to get directions and the okay to stop by.

They rode quietly for a while. Then Anya asked, "So this Duncan kid is a good friend of yours?"

Stella was startled. "No! Um, actually I don't really like him. He thinks he's funny, but he's not."

"Oh."

A few minutes later, Anya turned into the Crowes' bumpy driveway. They bounced along toward a shabby frame house that was brightly lit. Stella could see the blue glow from a TV screen in one of the front rooms. An enormous eighteen-wheeler was pulled up in the grass. Duncan's dad was home.

"There's Duncan," Stella said.

He was sitting on the porch. He got up and walked toward the truck as Anya turned off the engine.

Stella hopped out of the truck. "Aunt Anya, this is Duncan. Duncan, this is my aunt."

"So you want to see the most beautiful calf in the county, heh?" Duncan said.

Anya smiled. "If you don't mind."

"My pleasure! Right this way, please." He bowed deeply and gestured around the house.

They went around to the backyard.

"I call her Isa," Duncan said proudly.

Isa was lying under the pasture's only tree—a mountain ash with sprawling limbs. The calf was chewing her cud and calmly watching them approach. She was a holstein. Her fur was black and white in patches, with a white band running from her forehead down over her nose and mouth.

"Hi there, girl." Anya knelt down and ran her hand over Isa's side.

"Mmmmmrw," Isa said loudly.

"Stella told me Isa was off her feed," Anya said. Duncan nodded.

"Well, she looks well-nourished," Anya told him. "Her fur is shiny. Eyes bright. Looks to me

like she's getting plenty of food. What are her rations?"

"Six pounds of grain each day," Duncan said. "But she didn't finish it this morning. And hay."

"Do you leave her in the pasture during the day?" Anya asked.

"All the time," Duncan said.

Anya looked around the pasture. Stella followed her gaze, trying to take in the details. About five acres. The grass was brown in a few patches, but basically looked good. The land was surrounded by a low wooden fence. Parts of it had tumbled over.

"Well, Isa is probably doing a little grazing," Anya said. "And that's slowing down her appetite for hay and grain."

"Is that bad?" Duncan asked.

"Not necessarily," Anya said. "What's important is to know that Isa is growing fast enough. That will let you know if her diet is adequate."

Duncan was frowning. "What do I do? Take her in and put her on the bathroom scale?"

Anya cocked her head. "*That* might be difficult. But you can measure her." She got up and gave Duncan a pat on the back. "Come on, I have a hearth-girth tape out in the truck."

Stella followed Anya and Duncan out to the

truck and back. She stood around while Anya explained how to use the tape to measure Isa.

"Why don't you try it?" Anya suggested.

Duncan took the tape and made a stupid face. "Come on, Isa," he baby-talked. "Let's see how you measure up, sweetie. If you're a good little calf and stand still, maybe we'll get you a training bra."

Stella rolled her eyes. She didn't think Duncan should act like such a goof. Especially not when Anya was giving him so much of her time. The least he could do was show a little respect.

But Anya didn't seem to mind. She waited patiently while Duncan got the calf up and wrapped the tape around her shoulders. He stood staring at the numbers for a long time.

"What does it say?" Anya asked.

"Er . . . seventy-two centimeters," Duncan said.

"Okay," Anya said. "I want you to write that down somewhere. Then measure again tomorrow. Isa should grow every day. If she stops growing, or even slows down, then you have a problem."

"Sounds like homework," Duncan said.

"Maybe a little," Anya said.

Duncan brightened. "But it's worth it to win a blue ribbon at the county fair! What do you think, Ms. Goodwin? Do you think she could win?"

"That's going to depend on you," Anya said.

"She has good lines. But competition will be stiff. Only the biggest, healthiest calves will take home a ribbon."

"Isa and I aren't scared of a little competition," Duncan said with a swagger.

"There's something else I'm worried about," Anya told him. "Isa could get out of this fence if she wanted to. Even worse, a predator could get in."

Duncan's gaze moved to Stella. "Like one of Stella's wolves?" he asked.

Stella made a face at him. Duncan and some of the other kids at school were always teasing her about the wolves.

Big deal, Stella thought. She was proud to have helped bring the wolves back.

Gray wolves had once been abundant on the land that was now Goldenrock National Park. Two hundred years earlier, when Europeans first started arriving in the American West, the forests had been home to thousands of wolves.

Gradually, though, the European settlers had tamed the land. They put up fences, built railroads and towns, and brought in great herds of cattle and sheep.

The settlers' survival rested on the survival of their animals. So they hadn't felt too welcoming toward anything that had threatened their livestock. Wolves were one big threat, and the settlers had hunted them until they were completely wiped out.

Decades later, people began to notice changes in the forest. Animals the wolves had hunted were growing more and more numerous. Elk and deer were overgrazing certain plants.

People began to talk about bringing the wolves back. Norma and Jack and Anya supported the idea. And, when she got old enough, so did Stella.

They'd fought a long time. And just that summer, about a dozen wolves had been returned to the national park. One female had given birth to pups—the first Goldenrock wolf pups in seventy years.

Some people, mostly ranchers and farmers, thought the reintroduced wolves were dangerous. They felt the same way their great-great-great-grandparents had felt: that predators and livestock didn't mix. Josie, Stella's best friend, lived on a ranch and she thought that.

Other people seemed to think it was silly to get so excited about a dozen animals. Duncan was one of those.

"Watch out!" Duncan told Isa. "The big bad wolf is going to get you." He laughed at his own joke.

Anya smiled tolerantly. "The wolves could be

a threat, although I think that's unlikely. You'll probably get more trouble from panthers and coyotes. Do you think your dad would help you mend the fence?"

"Oh, sure," Duncan said, spinning the tape measure around over his head. "He should have some free time in, say, 2045."

"Works a lot, does he?" Anya asked.

"Only if you consider every single day 'a lot,'" Duncan said. "He drives from here to North Carolina and back every week. Do you know how far it is to North Carolina? Far, that's how far."

Anya nodded. She squinted at the darkening pasture. "And you leave Isa out here all night?"

"Sure. She's not afraid of wolves."

"Got a dog?"

"Nope."

"Maybe you should talk to your parents about getting one," Anya said. "Or a donkey. Donkeys are very good at guarding livestock against predators."

"A donkey. Oookaaay," Duncan said with a laugh.

"You don't sound worried," Stella said.

Josie's family had a huge cattle ranch and Josie was always worried about predators. Even though her family seemed to spend half their lives repairing fences.

Duncan shrugged. "My bedroom is right up there," he said, pointing. "I kept an eye on Isa all night long. No panther is going to get my blue-ribbon calf."

"Don't you sleep?" Stella asked.

"Actually, no. I'm a vampire! Bla-ha-ha!"

Anya gave Duncan a pat on the back. "Okay. Well, good luck."

"Bye!" Duncan called. "See you tomorrow, Stella. And don't be late!"

"Bye!" Stella trotted after her aunt. "He's pretty clueless, huh?" she asked.

"Completely," Anya said.

Stella was nervous the next morning.

The school year was two days old. She'd been late both days. Not a good record. Also, it was painfully clear to Stella that her new teacher didn't like her. She was going to have to earn Mrs. Orne's trust. Step one: be on time.

Stella crawled out of bed extra early. She rushed though her usual morning routine, thinking, *hurry, hurry, hurry.*

She shivered as she stepped out onto the back porch. The morning air was damp and chilly. The fall weather reminded her of John's deadline. She hoped he would heal in time to hibernate.

Stella pulled her bike out of the shed. She'd left herself a whole half-hour to drop Rufus off at the clinic and get to school.

The puppy was in her backpack. He seemed excited to be going for a ride. Maybe he thought Stella was taking him to school.

Stella got on her bike and pedaled down to the junction of Route 98. She waited while a big green delivery truck zipped by in the right lane. Then she turned onto the shoulder and headed into town.

She was thinking about Duncan and Isa. Even though Duncan had acted stupid the evening before, Stella was almost certain he was worried about Isa. Making awful jokes was just his way of coping. She wondered if she could help Duncan get a guard dog somewhere.

Stella pedaled past the POPULATION: 9,812 sign.

Maybe Aunt Anya knows someone who has puppies to give away, Stella thought as she rode on. *Or maybe I could call Papa Pete.* Papa Pete was her grandfather.

She rode around the bend.

But what are the chances? Stella wondered. Good guard dogs were in hot demand and hard to get. Especially free.

Almost as a reflex, Stella glanced toward the spot where she had found John.

She hit the brakes hard.

Something was ambling into the road, almost exactly where Stella had found the turtle.

It was a dog! A golden retriever with wet paws and matted fur. A car or truck coming around the bend wouldn't be able to see him.

"Hey! Puppy! Move!" Stella yelled, still straddling her bike.

The dog looked back at Stella and Rufus over one shoulder. Then he trotted a few feet farther into the road and paused to sniff at a spot of . . . something.

Stella climbed off her bike, feeling a rising sense of urgency. "Come here, boy!" she called.

The dog looked up for a moment, then went back to sniffing.

Stella hesitated. She wanted to pull the dog off the road. But what should she do with Rufus? It would be safer to put him down in case . . .

Well, just in case.

But then Rufus might try to run off. Or follow her. Could she tie his leash to her bike?

Yes, Stella thought. *Hurry!*

She slipped off her backpack and pulled Rufus out. With him tucked under one arm, she grabbed his leash out from inside the bag. She clipped the leash onto his collar. And then—

A low hum.

Ssssshhhhhhh.

A motor. The sound of wheels on pavement. Coming closer. Fast.

Stella turned toward the sound.

A truck was barreling around the bend. An enormous white truck with a big gleaming silver grill. Going at least fifty miles an hour. Stella couldn't see into the cab. Couldn't see the driver at all.

Did that mean he couldn't see her?

Stella dropped Rufus and yanked him back, away from the road. "Stop!" she yelled, waving her arms. She jumped up and down. "Stopstopstop. Please stop!"

The truck never even slowed down. It sped around the bend, blocking the dog from Stella's sight.

Stella let out a low moan. She held Rufus's leash, squeezed her eyes shut and prayed the retriever would get out of the way in time.

THUMP.

Stella cringed. She felt sick inside. That thump could mean only one thing. The truck had hit the dog.

She opened her eyes and saw the big square back of the truck. The brake lights came on for a split second and then went out. The truck continued down the road.

Stella was shaking, quivering. "What?" she screamed. "What's wrong with you? You can't just *leave!*"

She didn't want to look toward the street. But she *had* to look. What if another truck came along? And another truck *would* come along—and soon.

Stella forced her eyes toward the road.

The big yellow dog was lying there with his legs facing her. Lying completely still.

"Please be alive," Stella whispered. Her throat felt tight. It was hard to breathe.

Stella felt very alone.

How could the truck driver have just driven away?

What was she going to do?

A little voice inside her head answered. *Get the dog out of the road. Fast.*

Still clutching Rufus's leash, Stella ran into the road and made herself look down at the dog.

Rufus nudged the golden retriever's paw with his nose and whimpered. The golden didn't react. He was out cold.

Out cold . . . or dead.

Stella felt dizzy. Her hands were shaking, and she couldn't remember what to do. She wished her mom was with her. Or Anya.

Anya, Stella thought. *I've got to get the dog to Anya.*

Stella bent down and forced her hands under

the unconscious dog. Rufus danced out of the way and watched her curiously.

A thin line of blood was coming out of the golden's mouth. That wasn't good. Stella seemed to remember it was a sign of internal injuries.

Hurry.

The golden was big. Stella braced for the strain of picking him up. Put her back into it. But he wasn't that heavy.

A blue car was coming from the direction of town. The driver beeped.

Stella ran for the shoulder. She was holding the big dog and Rufus's leash.

Rufus trotted along at her heels, looking up at her.

"Come on, Ruf," Stella said. She started down the shoulder, her breath coming in gasps. She kept hearing that awful *thump* in her head.

Stella was scared. Scared the golden was dead. Scared she was doing something to hurt him. If his spine was broken . . . Maybe she shouldn't have moved him.

Don't think about that, Stella told herself. It was too late to change her decision. And besides, she couldn't have left the dog in the road.

She continued down the road. The scrubby, dirty plants that grew along the side scratched at her ankles. Cars and trucks kept going by.

Stella was angry. Angry that she had to carry this poor dog to the clinic. Why hadn't the driver stopped? Was he afraid to admit he'd killed a dog by driving carelessly? Or did he just not care?

She passed the gas station. The driver of an oversized sport utility vehicle with Colorado plates stared at her.

Okay, so she looked crazy carrying an unconscious, bleeding dog down the street. Well, so what?

Stella kept going. The golden was starting to feel heavy now. But Stella ignored the strain in her arms. All she cared about was getting to the clinic.

She passed the entrance to The Wooden Spoon. Kept going.

"Stella? Honey, is that you?"

It was Mrs. Crouse. She worked as a waitress at the diner. She was running across the parking lot in her waitress uniform, looking worried. Stella knew her kids—Pete and Maggie. And their cat, Missy.

"Stella, are you all right?" Mrs. Crouse came up to Stella's side.

Stella turned to her, suddenly feeling overwhelmed. "I'm okay. But someone hit this dog. He's hurt bad. I've got to get h–him to A-Aunt Anya."

"Okay, honey. Okay. I'm going to help you. I'm here. It's going to be all right. Why don't you give him to me?"

"I—I can't. I'm scared. If his back is broken or something, that might hurt him. I probably never should have picked him up. But he was lying in the middle of the road!"

"You did the right thing. I'm sure of it." Mrs. Crouse eased the leash out of Stella's hand and picked up Rufus. "Let me take Rufus. Come on, it's just another block to the clinic."

They started down the street together. Mrs. Crouse put her arm around Stella's back, supporting her.

Stella was still shaky, but having Mrs. Crouse there made her feel better. The dog was beginning to feel incredibly heavy. He was so limp.

Dead weight.

Stella picked up the pace. She was practically running. The sidewalk was a blur. Mrs. Crouse hurried along by her side. When they got to the clinic, Mrs. Crouse shot forward and opened the door. "Anya!" she called. "Come quick!"

Stella stumbled up the steps. The golden was definitely getting heavy.

Anya came out of her office. "Stella—what happened? Are you okay?"

"A truck hit this dog," Stella said. She was so

relieved to see her aunt that tears began to stream down her cheeks. She gasped for air. Suddenly she felt weak—like she was going to drop the golden. "What should I do with him?"

"Put him in Exam One," Anya said.

Stella stumbled into the room.

Anya helped her lay the dog gently on the exam table.

Mrs. Crouse followed them. She was holding one hand over her mouth and shaking her head. "Stella scared me to death," she told Anya. "I saw her walking past the diner with that poor bloody thing and I didn't know what to think!"

Anya put a hand on Mrs. Crouse's shoulder. "Thanks for coming in with her."

Mrs. Crouse put Rufus down.

Rufus immediately trotted over to Stella and stood staring up at her.

"Well, of *course*," Mrs. Crouse said. She gasped. "Goodness gracious! I've got four tables back at the diner. I'd better get back before their pancakes get cold."

"Thanks again," Anya said.

As soon as Mrs. Crouse was gone, Anya reached down and gave Stella a tight hug. "Are you okay?" she asked, pulling back.

"Um, yeah," Stella said, wiping at her eyes. She took a deep breath. "Is he going to be okay?"

"I need to take a look," Anya said. "But right now, I'm more worried about you."

"I'm fine."

"You're shaking."

"I—I was scared," Stella admitted. "But I feel better now. Please take care of the dog."

"Okay," Anya agreed. "But I want you to get a glass of water and sit down for a few minutes."

"Okay." Stella went to the sink and filled a paper cup with water. She took a small sip.

Rufus followed, trailing his leash. Stella picked him up and buried her face in his fur. Then she raised her eyes, watching her aunt from across the room.

Anya was examining the dog. Running her fingers over his fur, peering at his gums, lifting his eyelids. She didn't look happy.

"Well?" Stella asked.

Anya sighed. "Looks like a stray," she said vaguely.

"Yeah," Stella said. "No collar."

"No collar," Anya agreed. "Plus, he's skin and bones. Covered with fleas. Probably has worms."

Anya had stopped her exam. She was just standing with her arms crossed. Looking down at the dog sadly.

"What's the matter?" Stella demanded. "Why don't you do something?"

Anya rubbed her eyes. "Stella, this dog is in sorry shape." She spoke quietly. "His pelvis is broken. He's suffering from internal bleeding and shock. And he wasn't in good health to begin with."

"So?" Stella said, her voice rising. "Aren't you even going to *try* to save him?"

"I'm not sure that's the kindest thing." Anya looked tired and uneasy.

Stella felt a flash of anger. "Are you saying that the kindest thing is to let him *die?*"

"I'm saying we'd be putting the dog through a lot of pain by operating on him," Anya said. "Even if he lives, he'd have a lot of healing to do. And for what? We'd eventually have to take him to the pound. And, chances are, nobody would adopt him."

Stella didn't want to believe she'd heard right. Anya wanted to give up? Without even trying? And she thought that was being *kind?*

"I'll find a home for him," Stella said. "I *promise*. You've got to try to help him."

Anya looked at Stella for a moment. She seemed to take in her bloody shirt, her tear-streaked face. "Okay," she said with a tired smile. "I'll try. But—"

"Thank you, Aunt Anya!"

"*But* I can't promise he'll survive," Anya pressed on.

Stella gave her aunt a hug. "That's okay. Just do your best."

Anya moved toward the sink and started scrubbing her hands. "I will. Now, why don't you go upstairs, change your clothes and then get out of here?"

"Get out? Why?"

"Stella! School."

Stella said a word she wasn't supposed to say. Then she shot a guilty look at her aunt.

Anya chuckled. "Don't worry, I won't tell. Just go."

Stella did.

By the time Stella changed her clothes, went back for her bike, and rode to school, she was *seriously* late.

She eased the classroom door open and walked in as quietly as possible. Everyone immediately looked up. *Great,* Stella thought.

Marisa gave her a sympathetic smile. Josie looked relieved for a second, then worried. Jared shot a quick glance at Mrs. Orne.

The teacher slowly rose to her feet and peered down at Stella over her big black glasses. "Stella Sullivan," she said, slowly shaking her head. "This is the third day in a row you have been late. You *must* develop better habits."

Stella wanted to explain. But she knew what Mrs. Orne would say: No excuses.

"Sorry," Stella said bitterly.

She thought Mrs. Orne wasn't being fair. Okay, granted, being on time to school *was* important. But some things were even *more* important. And taking care of the golden was one of those things. Even though Stella had broken the rules, she didn't feel as if she'd done anything wrong.

Stella slipped into her seat and tried not to attract any more attention.

The school day passed slowly.

Stella kept thinking about the golden. Wondering if he was still alive. She knew Anya would do her best to save him. But sometimes animals were beyond saving, even with the best care.

Detention was the worst part of the day. By the time it rolled around, Stella was itching to leave the building. Itching to get away from Mrs. Orne. Itching to find out how the golden was doing.

He was going to live.

He *had* to.

And if he lived, Stella had to find him a home.

Maybe Norma and Jack would let Stella keep him. But that was doubtful. Stella remembered how her parents had reacted when she suggested getting another dog to keep Rufus company.

What about someone in her class?

Suddenly Stella thought about Duncan, who

was sitting a few desks away. His head was bent over his math workbook. He had a pencil in a death grip in his left hand.

Duncan needed a dog to guard Isa. The golden needed a home. Why not get them together?

It was perfect!

Of course, Stella had no idea if the golden would be a good guard dog. But at least he could bark if a panther strolled into the Crowes' yard. Assuming he lived. . . .

Stella decided to see how the golden was doing and then talk to Duncan about adopting him.

Feeling satisfied, she glanced up at the clock. Twenty-one minutes had gone by. Detention was supposed to be over a minute ago.

The minute hand clicked.

Make that two minutes ago.

Duncan and Stella exchanged desperate looks. Was Mrs. Orne ever going to let them go?

The teacher seemed to sense their stress. She looked up from her paperwork. "Duncan, you may go," she said. "Stella, I'd like to talk to you for a moment."

Duncan shot Stella a supportive look, grabbed his books, and fled. Stella picked up her things and slowly approached the teacher's desk.

"I wanted to tell you that I will be contacting

your parents this evening," Mrs. Orne said coolly. "I want to discuss your tardiness with them."

Stella fought a desire to roll her eyes. "Okay," she said sullenly. She wasn't worried. She knew Norma and Jack would understand why she'd been late.

"May I go now?" Stella asked.

"Yes," Mrs. Orne said. "I'll see you tomorrow."

Stella nodded and hurried out the door.

Three minutes later, she was walking into the clinic. Anya was on the phone, but she covered the mouthpiece long enough to tell Stella the golden was in the boarder room.

Yes! Stella thought. *He's still alive!* She gave Anya a grateful smile and rushed down the hallway. Rufus bounded out of the office and trotted after her.

The boarder room was filled with different-sized cages. Anya kept animals there while they recovered from surgery or waited for their owners to pick them up.

John, the turtle, was in a large aquarium near the corner of the room. He was moving around a little. A piece of parsley was hanging out of his mouth. Stella was glad to see he was eating.

The golden retriever was in a low cage. He was asleep on a pad, stretched out on one side. He seemed too limp—as if he were so deeply asleep that his muscles had lost all of their tone.

Stella knew the dog was whacked out from the drugs Anya had used to put him out for surgery. But still . . . he looked weak. His breaths were shallow. Like he might stop breathing any second.

"Hi there, sweetie," Stella cooed. She sat down on the concrete floor in front of the cage and pushed the door open. The golden's lower abdomen was shaved and elaborately bandaged. He smelled of antiseptic and flea powder.

Stella gently petted the soft orangish fur on his front leg. "Hi," she said huskily. "You've had a really rough day, eh? Well, don't worry. You're okay now. We're going to take care of you. Everything is going to be okay."

Rufus lowered himself down on his haunches. He rested his furry head on Stella's knee and let out a low moan.

Stella smiled and scratched Rufus behind his ears. "Don't freak, Ruf. The golden is going to get better. You'll see."

Rufus and Stella stayed in front of the cage until Stella's legs went numb and her stomach rumbled with hunger. Finally, she got up to stretch and see if Anya had something to eat. Rufus followed along at her heels.

Stella found Anya in Exam Two, cleaning a terrier's teeth.

Rufus was suddenly hyperalert. "Ruf! Rufrufruf!" he barked at the other dog.

"Shh," Stella said sternly.

Rufus stopped barking. But now the terrier was squirming to get down and get acquainted with Rufus.

Anya was not amused. "Stella, please take Rufus into the office," she said testily.

"Sure," Stella said. She scooped the little dog up and put him in the office. She went back to Exam Two. The terrier was still on the table.

Anya was working on his molars. "How's the golden?" she asked as she continued to scrape away.

"Still asleep."

Anya sighed. "He's so weak."

"I know," Stella said, feeling a prick in her heart. "Even Rufus seems to know."

"Hmm," Anya said with a tight frown.

"What's the matter?"

Anya heaved another sigh. "Well, Rufus was quite a *presence* here today. He made himself a pest, barking at all of my patients."

Stella's heart sank. She shook her head sadly. "What has gotten into him lately?"

"I don't know. But I can't have him upsetting

animals that are already sick or stressed." Anya put down her instrument and gave the terrier a pat on the head. "I'll keep him through the end of the week," she said. "But then you'll have to come up with another solution."

"Okay," Stella whispered. *Another solution— like what?* she wondered.

Rufus couldn't stay inside. He couldn't stay outside. He couldn't stay at the clinic. And he certainly couldn't come to school with Stella. What other options were there?

The phone rang.

"Could you get that?" Anya asked. "I want to get this little guy settled and check on the golden."

"No problem." Stella jogged to the office and grabbed the phone. "Goodwin Animal Clinic," she said.

"Oh. Um . . . hi. That Anya?" It was a man's voice and he sounded uneasy.

"No, this is Stella. I'm Anya's niece. She can't come to the phone right now. May I give her a message?"

"Well, all right." There was a long, considering pause. "Tell her to get on out to the Crowes' house."

The Crowes? Was this Duncan's father? Why would he be calling? Was he mad Anya had come out to look at Isa? Or was something wrong with the calf?

"May I tell her what the problem is?" Stella asked.

"Just tell her to get out here right away," Mr. Crowe said. And then the phone went dead.

• 10 •

Stella ran back to the boarder room and told Anya about Mr. Crowe's call. She emphasized how completely creeped out he sounded.

Anya didn't hesitate. She grabbed her jacket and keys, locked up, and hustled toward her 4 x 4.

"Can I come?" Stella called. She still had an hour before dinner.

"Sure! Climb in."

Stella quickly shut Rufus and Boris into Anya's office. In the truck, Anya wasted no time. She started it up, put her foot on the gas and headed down 98 toward Route 2A. Stella snapped in her seat belt and stared out the window.

The sky was powder blue, cloudless. The sun was just falling toward the horizon and it looked almost like an enormous orange hole. The light was golden. Everything was throwing long shadows—buildings, trucks, cows in the pastures they passed; even the grass.

Anya bounced into the Crowes' yard.

Stella got a weird feeling right off. Something seemed wrong. All of the lights in the house were on—even though it wasn't even dark outside.

"Looks like everyone is on the porch," Anya said as she pulled to a stop.

Anya and Stella climbed out of the truck and approached the house.

A woman with a long, gray ponytail was sitting on an old, low rocking chair. Duncan's younger sister—her name was Pippa, Stella knew somehow—was sitting on one of the chair's arms and huddling close to her mom. Duncan was standing right behind them, his arms wrapped around his chest.

As Stella and Anya walked up, Mr. Crowe came out the screen door. He was a wiry man with a buzz cut.

From a few yards away, Stella could see that Duncan and Pippa were crying. Duncan didn't even try to hide it. Mrs. Crowe looked glum and her husband wasn't smiling.

"Hey there," Anya called heartily. "I heard you folks needed my help."

Mr. Crowe looked at Stella for a long moment, then shifted his gaze to Anya. He didn't answer.

Stella shifted her weight uneasily. She didn't exactly feel *welcome*. But if Mr. Crowe hadn't wanted Anya to come, why had he called?

"Is something wrong with Isa?" Anya tried again.

Mr. Crowe nodded. "Something got her," he muttered low.

Anya processed that for a moment. "Where is she?" she asked.

"Out back."

Anya started to jog around the corner of the house.

Stella hesitated for a moment, then followed her aunt. Her heart was thump-thumping. Judging from the expressions on the Crowes' faces, what she was about to see wouldn't be pretty.

Something got Isa. . . .

What did that mean?

Anya had come to a stop under the same tree where she had examined Isa the evening before. The calf was lying on her side.

Stella could see a couple of black and white legs, but she couldn't see what was wrong with the calf. Anya was in the way. Stella moved a few feet to the right so that she had a better view.

Anya suddenly realized she was there. "Stella—don't!" she warned.

Too late.

Stella had seen.

Seen that Isa's belly was split open almost as if someone had used a knife to cut it. Something white and spongy was spilling out of the red gaping hole in her gut. One leg was mostly down to bone. Flies were buzzing around.

"Oh," Stella moaned. She closed her eyes and covered her mouth. She had never seen anything so awful. Never imagined it.

Still, her mind instantly made sense of what she was seeing: Something had been *eating* Isa.

Anya put her hands on Stella's shoulders and turned her back toward the house. "Go," she said.

Dizzy, stumbling, Stella ran back toward the porch.

Something had killed Isa. Killed her and then *ate* her. What could do that?

Something big.

A predator. Or a group of predators. Like, like . . .

A wolf.

The thought stopped Stella. She stood staring at the grass in the Crowes' side yard without really seeing it. Her stomach did a slow turn.

A wolf.

Stella could see the scene in her mind. One of her precious wolves had come bounding out of the woods. Isa was just standing there like a dumb cow, chewing her cud. She didn't even react as the gnashing teeth, the powerful paws pulled her down.

A wolf . . . doing what wolves do. Killing weaker animals and *eating* them.

Stella's blood chilled.

She thought of all the times she'd self-righteously told Josie that Goldenrock *needed* wolves. Josie always said that ranchers had a responsibility to protect their livestock—and that meant no wolves. No wolves—even though they were a natural part of the Goldenrock ecosystem. Stella didn't think she had ever really heard Josie's arguments. But now she understood.

Stella went around to the porch and sank down on the steps. Her knees were weak. She didn't say anything to the Crowes—couldn't—and they didn't say anything to her.

This is my fault, Stella thought. *If I hadn't fought so hard for the wolf reintroduction, this never would have happened.*

Anya came around the house. She walked past Stella up the porch steps. She stopped in front of the rocking chair, facing all of the Crowes.

"Isa is dead," Anya told them quietly. "There's

nothing I can do for her now except help you bury her."

Mr. Crowe stirred. "I'll get the shovels," he said gruffly.

Anya nodded.

He clumped down the steps and headed around back.

Pippa sniffled. "Wh–what got her?"

"A coyote," Anya said. "But don't be scared. Coyotes don't like little girls."

Pippa gave her a shy smile.

A coyote! Stella turned this information over in her mind, hardly believing it. A coyote had killed Isa. Not a wolf.

Mr. Crowe came back and Anya went out back with him. Mrs. Crowe heavily got to her feet and went inside.

Pippa, Duncan, and Stella stayed on the porch. They were quiet. Just watching the sun sink below the horizon. The sky was turning orange and purple. It was beautiful, which made Stella sad for some reason.

Faintly Stella could hear the sound of digging.

A coyote had killed Isa. Not a wolf.

Somehow knowing that didn't make Stella feel relieved. Isa was still dead.

Another thought hit Stella like a punch to the gut. With Isa dead, the Crowes wouldn't need a guard dog. Stella would have to find someone else to adopt the golden. That didn't seem right. Isa and the golden had seemed made for each other.

Twenty minutes later, Anya came back. She was sweating and dirt clung to her face. "Ready to go?" she asked Stella.

"Ready."

They said good-bye quietly. Then walked over to the truck and climbed in.

"How do you know it was a coyote?" Stella asked. She couldn't shake her fear that it had actually been a wolf.

"The characteristics of the kill," Anya said. "Coyotes are the only animals that are so neat about opening up their prey." She turned and looked at Stella for a moment. "Why?"

"I was thinking about the wolves."

Anya nodded. She understood. Understood that Stella had just confronted a fact she'd been avoiding for a long time. Wolves were predators. Just like coyotes. Goldenrock's ecosystem might need them. But that didn't change the fact that they were killers.

• 11 •

That evening, Stella wrote another letter to the *Gateway Gazette*.

Dear Editor,
*   The bend in Route 98 just before the town line is extremely dangerous. This morning, I watched a delivery truck hit a golden retriever on that patch of road.*
*   The driver didn't even stop.*
*   The dog suffered a broken pelvis, shock, and internal bleeding. Anya Goodwin is treating him, but he may not live.*
*   Please tell people to slow down.*
*   Sincerely,*
*   Stella Sullivan*

She printed out the letter and took it into the kitchen for Jack to read. He was standing at the sink, rinsing dishes. He had the phone cradled between his shoulder and ear.

"I'm sorry she's been a disruption," Jack said. He put the last plate into the dishwasher and turned off the water. "Stella is actually a very responsible kid."

Oh, great, Stella thought. She sank down at the kitchen table. Mrs. Orne was calling her parents just like she'd threatened to. Well, at least Jack was standing up for her. Maybe Mrs. Orne would listen to him.

Jack raised his eyebrows at Stella, acknowledging her presence. "I'm sure she wouldn't be late without a good reason," he said into the phone.

Uh-oh. Mrs. Orne wasn't going to like *that.* Sure enough, Jack furrowed his brow and started nodding slowly. Stella was almost certain Mrs. Orne was giving him a lecture.

"I see," Jack said, a bit testily. "Well, we'll make sure Stella is on time tomorrow." A pause. "Yes, yes, and every day after that. I understand. Good-bye."

Jack turned off the phone and turned to Stella with a sigh. "She's mean," he said.

"That's what I keep telling everyone!"

Jack pointed the phone at her. "Still, you know what you have to do."

Stella hung her head. "I know."

"Come on," Jack said. "Head up to bed now. I'll wake you up extra early."

"All right," Stella said.

She left the letter for Jack and went upstairs to bed.

It was *painfully* early when she climbed out from under the covers the next morning.

The rest of her family was still eating breakfast as Stella pulled her bike out of the shed. She had left herself a whole forty-five minutes to drop Rufus off at the clinic and get to school. She had *oceans* of time. Nothing could possibly make her late.

Still, Stella felt apprehensive as she passed the town line and rounded the dangerous bend on Route 98.

Please let it be okay today, Stella prayed.

And, to her surprise, it was okay. No animals were lying in the road. None were wandering in. They were probably all still asleep.

Stella continued into town and pulled up to the clinic. She dropped her bike in the grass and hurried up the stairs. Anya had offered to keep Rufus for the rest of the week and Stella had to take her up on it. She still hadn't thought of anything else she could do with the puppy.

The front door of the clinic was locked. Stella let herself in with her key.

Boris came out of the office to greet her. But there was no sign of Anya. Stella could hear water running upstairs. Anya must still be in the shower. Man, it was *early*.

Stella put Rufus down. Boris touched noses with the puppy, saying a quick hello.

"I should go," Stella told the dogs. But the thought of getting to school before the *teachers*—before the *janitor* even—wasn't very appealing. Stella hesitated. "Maybe I'll just see how everyone is doing. I have plenty of time for that."

Stella made a quick detour into the boarder room. Rufus and Boris both followed along.

First the turtle. John looked about the same. He was just sort of hanging out. Healing, Stella hoped. Anya had left him plenty of clean water.

Stella crossed over to the golden. He was awake, watching her with eyes that looked sad and confused. "Hi, sweetie," Stella said. "How are you feeling this morning?"

The golden's tail moved. One quick wag. Then he put his head down on his paws and sighed. He seemed depressed.

Rufus moved around Stella. He put his nose up to the wire cage, sniffing eagerly.

The golden raised his head and cocked it to one side. He tried to scoot closer to the gate and get a better smell of the puppy, but it was difficult with his bandages.

"Do you want to make friends?" Stella asked. Neither dog seemed aggressive. Both were just curious.

Stella unlocked the cage door. Rufus trotted

through and put his nose to the golden's. The big dog's head was about the same size as the puppy's whole body.

The phone rang. Anya still hadn't come downstairs, so Stella ran into the office and picked it up. She half expected it to be Norma or Jack reminding her to be on time for school.

"Goodwin Animal Clinic."

"Stella?"

"Yes?"

"It's Bud. Bud from the gas station. I—I need help. Something terrible is wrong with Freddy. He's shaking and it's like he can't stop."

Freddy the ferret. Stella remembered him. He had cancer. Needed an operation.

"Hang on, Bud," Stella said. "I'm going to get Anya. Everything is going to be okay. Just hang on."

Stella put the receiver down on Anya's desk. She turned. Ran.

Bam! She knocked her head against something hard. What? Oh—Anya's head.

"Whoa!" Anya said, putting a hand to her forehead. "What's going on? Why the rush?"

"Phone! It's Bud. Freddy is in trouble."

Anya nodded and moved to pick up the phone, still rubbing her head. "Bud? What's happening?"

Stella hovered in the doorway, feeling sick inside. Bud sounded so scared. It must be awful to see a pet you loved for so long get sick. Really, really sick.

Anya was listening carefully. "Freddy is having a seizure," she said calmly after a moment. "His blood sugar is dangerously low. This is what I want you to do. Do you have some Karo syrup? No? How about honey? Good. Good, that's fine. Put some honey on your finger and rub it on Freddy's gums. Do it now. I'll hold."

Stella and Anya waited tensely. A few minutes later, Bud came back to the phone.

"Is he really?" Anya said with a smile. "That's great."

Stella let out her breath. It sounded as if the honey had helped.

"Yes," Anya was saying into the phone. "I'll be here all day. But you understand I can't do much for Freddy except operate. Did you . . . I see. Okay, then, bring Freddy in right away. I'll do the operation this afternoon."

Anya hung up the phone, still looking worried.

"Bud decided to go ahead with the operation?" Stella asked.

"Yup."

"So what's the matter?"

"Oh, nothing," Anya said. She gave Stella a smile. "I was just wishing I had some ferret blood on hand. Freddy has a long operation ahead of him. It would be easier on him if he could have a transfusion."

"Can't you get some?"

"I'm going to try," Anya said. "Best thing would be to find a healthy ferret to give Freddy a donation."

"Can I help?"

"No, you can't!" Anya said with a laugh. She pointed to the clock on her desk. "School starts in five minutes."

Stella started. How had it gotten so late? She'd left home in plenty of time. Norma and Jack would be furious if she was late again. Not to mention Mrs. Orne.

"Okay—see you later," Stella said quickly. "Rufus is around here somewhere. Back in the boarder room."

"Okay." Anya was flipping through her day planner. She gave Stella a brief smile, and then picked up the phone.

Stella ran for her bike.

• 12 •

The bell clanged just as Stella turned her bike into the school yard. The playground was empty. Stella saw an older kid fling open the door and run inside.

"I'm coming, I'm coming," she muttered.

She dumped her bike into the rack, grabbed her backpack and ran. She dashed into the classroom just as Mrs. Orne was closing the door.

"You're late," Mrs. Orne said.

Stella pointed to the clock, which still read 8:20. "Not technically," she said breathlessly. She gave Mrs. Orne a pleading look.

Mrs. Orne looked stormy, but she stepped aside to let Stella in. "You may sit down," she said.

"Actually, I wanted to ask you a question," Stella said.

Mrs. Orne raised her heavy eyebrows. "Yes?" she said, peering at Stella over her glasses.

"May I make an announcement to the class?" Stella asked. "It's important."

Mrs. Orne gave Stella a cool, appraising stare. She looked . . . curious, Stella thought. "Be my guest," she said, gesturing toward the front of the room.

Stella stepped in front of the teacher's desk.

Her classmates had settled into their seats. Jared was sitting in his front-row seat, right in front of Stella. Duncan was slumped down, looking depressed. Poor Duncan. He had to feel terrible about Isa. Marisa gave Stella a surprised smile. Josie had a guarded look on her face—as if she were worried about what Stella was up to now.

"Hi everybody," Stella began. "I guess most of you know that my Aunt Anya is a vet."

Lots of the kids nodded. At some point Anya had probably doctored an animal for each and every one of them. She was very well-known in Gateway.

"This afternoon Anya is going to operate on a ferret named Freddy," Stella continued. "He belongs to Bud—the guy from the gas station."

More nods of recognition. Apparently, Bud was well-known in town, too.

"Freddy needs some ferret blood to help him through the operation," Stella went on. "So if any of you own a ferret that could donate, please let me know."

Stella looked out over the sea of faces. Everyone looked glum. She immediately knew her classmates couldn't help. Her shoulders slumped. She'd wanted to help Freddy.

"Well, thanks anyway . . . ," Stella said sadly.

She felt a hand on her shoulder.

Stella turned. Mrs. Orne was right behind her, and she had a strange look on her face. It almost looked like . . . a smile.

"I think I can help," Mrs. Orne said.

"You own a ferret?" Stella demanded.

"Two," Mrs. Orne said proudly. "Buttercup and Violet."

"Oh," Stella said, trying to hide her shock. Mrs. Orne had pets? Named *Violet* and *Buttercup?* Maybe she wasn't that mean, after all. "Well, great. I'll tell you how to get to the clinic after school."

"After *detention,*" Mrs. Orne corrected.

"Right," Stella said.

Maybe you could have pets and still be mean.

But Stella needed Mrs. Orne's help. So did Freddy. So Stella spent detention drawing Mrs. Orne a map to the clinic. When they left school,

Mrs. Orne headed home to get Violet and Buttercup. Stella rode to the clinic on her bike.

Anya was preparing for surgery when Stella got there. She was excited to hear about the blood donation.

"Mrs. Orne should be here any minute," Stella said.

Anya gave her a wink. "I'm looking forward to meeting her," she said. "Come in back while we wait. I want to show you something before I start operating."

Stella followed Anya into the boarder room and over to the golden's cage.

The first thing Stella noticed was Rufus. He was inside the cage! Curled up in the middle of the golden's massive front legs. He lifted his head in greeting.

So did the golden.

Stella could see the change in the big dog. He was obviously still weak from his injuries. But he seemed perkier. The half-dead look had gone out of his eyes. For the first time, Stella felt certain that he was going to live.

"Has Rufus been in there all day?" Stella asked.

Anya nodded, looking proud and amazed. "Totally quiet. Totally focused. Like a good little nurse."

"No barking?"

"None. He's been too busy licking that abrasion behind the golden's ear."

"The golden looks better, doesn't he?"

"He's out of danger," Anya said with a nod. "And I think his new little friend helped a lot."

"Wow," Stella said, standing up a little taller. "Wow." After all the trouble Rufus had caused that week, it was nice to hear something positive about him. Now she knew how Norma and Jack felt when she brought home a good report card.

"I changed my mind," Anya said.

"What about?"

"About Rufus," Anya said. "I want to keep him at the clinic while you're at school."

"You don't have to—"

"I *want* to," Anya said. "I think he's going to be useful. He's developing a healing touch. Maybe he takes after you."

"Sure," Stella said proudly. "I can let you do that."

They heard a knock on the door.

"That must be Mrs. Orne," Stella said.

"She's right on time," Anya said.

Stella laughed. "Somehow I think she always is."

The next morning was Saturday.

Stella was looking forward to sleeping in after the hard week at school. But Norma shook her awake just after seven o'clock.

"Phone for you," she said sleepily.

"Who is it?" Stella asked.

Norma didn't answer. She was already walking, zombielike, back to bed.

Stella picked up the phone Norma had dropped near her feet. "Hello?"

"Hi, Stella. I need you to get over here right away." It was Anya.

Stella instantly felt more awake. "Why? What's up? Is there an emergency?"

Anya yawned. "Sort of," she said. "My phone has been ringing off the hook all morning."

Stella was still half asleep. She wasn't following. "You want me to answer your phone?"

"Well, the calls are for *you*," Anya said with a chuckle. "Actually, they're for the golden."

"Why would people call a dog on the phone?"

"Your letter to the editor came out in this morning's paper," Anya said.

Stella was still confused. "So?"

"*So* the golden is a celebrity," Anya said. "Half the people in the county want to adopt him."

"Hey—that's great," Stella said. "I'll be right over!"

"Thanks," Anya said. Then she hung up.

Stella hurried back into her room and began pulling clothes out of her closet. She was starting to feel more awake. It wasn't *that* early. About the same time she'd get up for school.

She was jazzed that the golden was going to get a good home. He deserved it after all he had been through. All in all, it hadn't been *such* a bad week. Well, there was nothing good about what had happened to Isa. But the golden had survived. And Freddy had pulled through the operation.

Long-sleeved T-shirt or a sweater? Stella wondered. She put her hand on the windowpane to see how cold it was outside. Cold. Sweater, definitely.

Stella went to her closet and started to dig through the piles of summer clothes, looking for something warmer to wear.

Suddenly she thought about John. She pulled out a favorite red sweater, feeling sad.

John wasn't going to heal in time to hibernate. Stella somehow just *knew*. The temperature was dropping too quickly. The turtle was going to be stuck inside all winter. Anya and Stella would have to fight to keep him alive until spring.

It's not right, Stella thought bitterly. Nobody had cared when John got hit. But everyone was anxious to rush to the golden's rescue.

She was happy the golden was going to have a good home—that wasn't it. But she just didn't understand why people didn't care about animals that weren't cute.

KEEP YOUR PETS SAFE

In this story, a cat eats a single Tylenol and almost dies. Why? Because her owner didn't know that small amounts of "people drugs" can be deadly to animals. What other common household items could be dangerous for your pets? Read on to find out.

Pet poisons

- **Human medications** such as aspirin, ibuprofen, Tylenol, cold medicines, and vitamins can be deadly for animals. **Prevention tips:** Never give your pet drugs designed for humans unless prescribed by a veterinarian. Keep medications on a high shelf where pets can't reach them. Remember that dogs can chew into childproof pill bottles and tubes of ointment.

- **Dog medications** may be dangerous to cats and ferrets—and the reverse can be true, too. **Prevention tip:** Don't give your pet any drug unless the vet says it's a good idea.
- **Garbage**—especially rotting meat—often contains bacteria (tiny living cells). Certain kinds of bacteria can make animals very sick. **Prevention tip:** Don't let your pets roam outside where they can snack on garbage and roadkill.
- Drano, Ajax, toilet-bowl cleaners, pine oils, soap, bleach, dishwasher detergent, and other **cleaning products** can cause severe burns of animals' tongues, mouths, and stomachs. **Prevention tip:** Put pet-proof latches on storage areas, or keep cleaners where your pets can't reach them.
- Mouse or roach **traps** contain sweet-smelling ingredients that can attract pets like dogs, cats, ferrets, and guinea pigs. **Prevention tip:** Ban these poisons from your home and yard, or at least make sure traps are set where your pets can't get at them.

- A single pan of **chocolate** brownies can kill a small dog! That is because chocolate is a canine poison. **Prevention tip:** Never feed dogs chocolate "treats." Stick with snacks developed for doggie digestive tracts. Dogs love sweet treats so make sure to store chocolate out of your dog's reach. Be especially careful during Halloween!

- Other **foods** that can be dangerous for small animals: coffee grounds, onions, onion powder, tea, salt, macadamia nuts, and avocados. Animals sometimes eat **nonfood items**, too. Mothballs, potpourri, homemade play dough, fabric softener sheets, batteries, and cigarettes are all highly toxic to animals. **Prevention tip:** Store these products in places your pet can't reach.

- **Antifreeze,** a chemical used in cars, has a sweet taste. Many animals—particulary cats—are poisoned when they lick up antifreeze spills. Even small quantities can cause severe damage to an animal's kidneys. **Prevention tip:** Always supervise your dogs, ferrets, and bunnies when they're outside. Consider keeping your cat indoors.

- **Fertilizers, herbicides,** or **insecticides** can harm pets—especially small ones like birds and guinea pigs. **Prevention tip:** Learn to live with bugs and weeds in places your pet plays. Never let your pets walk on yards that have been recently treated with any of these chemicals.
- Nibbling on some **common plants** can be fatal for pets. Azalea, wax begonia, rhododendron, oleander, mistletoe, sago palm, yew, or lilies can all be dangerous. **Prevention tip:** Study up so you can recognize these plants when you see them. Remove any dangerous plants from your home or garden.
- **Flea collars, dips, and sprays** can cause problems if pet owners don't follow the directions on the label. **Prevention tip:** Ask your veterinarian to recommend a flea treatment. Never use products designed for dogs on cats or products designed for cats on dogs. Always get an adult to help you with flea treatments and make sure you read the label carefully.
- **House paint, varnish,** and **stains** can make pets sick. **Prevention tip:** Keep pets out of the area when anyone is using these products in your home.

What to do if your pet is poisoned

1. Relax. You can help your pet more if you are cool and calm.
2. Try to figure out what poison is making your animal sick.
3. Call your veterinarian for help. You should have the phone number posted near the phone.
4. Tell an adult to bring a sample of the poison—like a portion of cleanser still in the container or a plant clipping—with you to the vet. Seeing the poison will help the veterinarian treat your animal.

Emily Costello, the author of the *Animal Emergency* series, would like to hear from you. Send her an e-mail at emily@enarch-ma.com or write to her care of HarperCollins Children's Books.